Walt Disney's

DuckTales

The Secret City
Under the Sea

By Paul S. Newman

Illustrated by Bill Langley and Annie Guenther

A GOLDEN BOOK · NEW YORK

Western Publishing Company, Inc., Racine, Wisconsin 53404

MCMXCI

One lazy summer day Scrooge McDuck was reading an article in the *Duckburg Times* while his three nephews played a game. Suddenly Scrooge interrupted the quiet with a shout. "A gold coin has been found on Duckburg Beach!" he said.

"Where did it come from?" asked Dewey as the nephews gathered around Scrooge.

"Nobody knows," said Scrooge. "The only clue is the engraving on the coin. It says, 'Atlantis, 1888 A.S.' Now, I wonder what that means?"

"Let's look Atlantis up in our *Junior Woodchuck Guide*," said Huey. The boys raced off to get the book.

Louie read aloud from the guide. "No one knows if Atlantis ever really existed or if it is just a legend. Atlantis is said to be an island whose inhabitants created a very advanced scientific kingdom. Centuries ago Atlantis suddenly sank into the ocean to become a fabulous undersea city rich in gold, but no one has ever discovered exactly where it is located."

"Rich in gold!" Scrooge's eyes lit up. "But what does '1888 A.S.' mean?"

"Maybe it means '1888 years after sinking,'" Louie suggested.

"Do you think Atlantis still exists, Uncle Scrooge?" asked Dewey.

"I must find out," said Scrooge. "If Atlantis exists, it must have gold!"

Scrooge and the boys went to the daring
inventor Gyro Gearloose for help in searching out
Atlantis.

"Well," Gyro said thoughtfully, "if this Atlantis is
underwater, I'd better make you a deep-sea
submarine."

After two hours of hammering and fitting metal
pieces together, Gyro declared that the sub was
ready to go.

The boys helped Scrooge haul a heavy sack into the *Atlantis Explorer.* The sack was filled with gold, in case they ran into any unusual expenses along the way to Atlantis.

Gyro sealed the hatch and started the engine. The sub dived beneath the water. The undersea adventure had begun!

They plunged down into the dark depths of the sea. Strange fish darted around them. The deeper they dived, the darker and more mysterious the sea grew.

"Turn on the spotlight," Scrooge said to Gyro.

"Aye-aye," said Gyro as he snapped on the spotlight control.

ZAP! ZAP! Explosions burst out in front of the sub.

Instead of a light bulb, Gyro had mistakenly put a laser into the spotlight. Its powerful beam was blowing up rocks and shells on the seabed. Gyro quickly found the switch and turned it off.

As the water cleared, the crew looked out the sub's porthole and gasped.

It was Atlantis! The famed city of ancient legend lay there glowing under a giant clear dome that rested on the sea floor.

Inside the dome was a fantastic and glorious world.

Gyro guided the sub into an air lock. They all climbed out of the sub and passed through the air lock into the city.

Scrooge ran ahead of the others. He saw glittering piles of gold all around. He rushed from one gold pile to another, shouting, "Gold! Genuine gold!"

Suddenly two burly ducks in uniform commanded, "Surrender, all aliens!"

"Surrender?" said Scrooge as the two guards yanked him away from a pile of gold. "Why do we have to surrender?"

"Be quiet! You are now King Lod's prisoners," one guard said as he confiscated Scrooge's bag of gold.

They were taken to King Lod's palace. The king
held up Scrooge's bag of gold. "You must have
plenty more of this where you come from," he said
to Scrooge.

Scrooge refused to answer the king.

"Very well," said King Lod. "Perhaps a little stay
in prison will give you time to think of your answer.
Take them away!" he ordered the guards.

The guards led the explorers to the basement of the palace. They opened a heavy door and locked the crew in a gloomy prison cell.

"Let me apologize for the rude welcome," said an elderly duck sitting in a corner of the cell. "This never would have happened when I was the king of Atlantis."

"You were the king of Atlantis?" Huey asked.

"Yes," said the elderly duck. "My name is King Gladone."

Then he told them the amazing history of this ancient city under the sea.

"Thousands of years ago," King Gladone began, "Atlantis sank beneath the sea. Luckily there were brilliant scientists who discovered a way to make artificial air by using pure gold and underwater elements. This machine here produces all the air for Atlantis.

"In order to maintain the air-making process, we Atlanteans must keep mining gold."

King Gladone continued. "Only the king was trusted with the secret air-making formula. During my rule a man named Lod captured me one night and hid me in this cell.

"The Atlanteans thought I was dead. Lod said that he had the air-making formula, so they had to name him king. Then evil times began for Atlantis....

"Now King Lod makes everyone work harder and harder searching for gold," King Gladone said sadly. "He wants more gold for himself to make gold crowns and jewels, and he leaves just enough so that we can keep breathing.

"But I have refused to give him the secret formula, which is why he keeps me alive. I am the only person in the world who knows how to run this machine."

"I wish we could help you," said Scrooge, "but there doesn't seem to be any way out of this place."

"I know," said King Gladone. "But I'm afraid King Lod will soon use up all the gold, and our city will be destroyed."

Suddenly Scrooge had an idea. "Maybe Gyro's spotlight on the sub can help us," he said.

"But it's not really a spotlight, Uncle Scrooge," said Louie. "It's a laser."

"Yes," said Scrooge, "but King Lod doesn't know that!"

Then Scrooge banged on the door and called to the guards. "Tell King Lod that I'm ready to get the gold he wants," Scrooge said.

The guards relayed the message to King Lod, and then they returned for Scrooge. "You may go and get the gold," the guards said, "but the rest of your crew shall remain here as hostages until you return."

Scrooge guided the sub out of the air lock. As soon as the sub was in the water, Scrooge switched on the laser. He aimed its penetrating beam on the giant dome over Atlantis.

ZAP! ZAP! The beam burned a hole in the dome.

"The dome is leaking!" cried the Atlanteans. Everyone panicked and began to run away. King Lod shouted orders as his guards tried to stop the water from flooding the city.

While the guards were busy repairing the leak,
Scrooge sneaked the sub back into Atlantis.

Scrooge dashed back to the prison. He found
the key to the cell and opened the door, releasing
Gyro and the nephews and a grateful King Gladone.

"Now we must capture King Lod and save the
people of Atlantis," said Scrooge. "Follow me, boys!"

As they walked toward the palace the crowds
went wild.

"Look!" someone cried. "It's King Gladone. He's
alive!"

When all the Atlanteans saw their beloved former
king, they cheered. Then they overpowered King
Lod and his guards and threw them in prison.

After making sure the leak was repaired, King Gladone mounted his gold throne. "How can I ever thank you?" he asked Scrooge.

With a big grin Scrooge looked at the piles of gold nearby.

"Oh, I'm sorry, Scrooge," said King Gladone, "but we need all our gold in order to keep breathing. You understand, don't you?"

Scrooge nodded his head as his own bag of gold was returned to him.

Back in Duckburg, Scrooge stared at his sack of gold. "This is all I have to show for all that trouble— and it's the gold I already had!"

"But we did have an exciting adventure, Uncle Scrooge," said Dewey.

"And we rescued the people of Atlantis from King Lod," added Huey.

"We certainly did," Scrooge agreed. "And that's the best reward ever!"